Giant Octopus to the Rescue

adapted by Alison Inches

based on a teleplay by Ligiah Villalobos

illustrated by Art Mawhinney

Ready-to-Read

Simon Spotlight/Nickelodeon

New York   London   Toronto   Sydney

Based on the TV series *Go, Diego, Go!*™ as seen on Nick Jr.®

SIMON SPOTLIGHT
An imprint of Simon & Schuster Children's Publishing Division
1230 Avenue of the Americas, New York, New York 10020

Manufactured in the United States of America
First Edition
2 4 6 8 10 9 7 5 3 1
Library of Congress Cataloging-in-Publication Data
Inches, Alison.
Giant octopus to the rescue / adapted by Alison Inches ; based on the teleplay by Ligiah Villalobos ;
illustrated by Art Mawhinney.
—1st ed.
p. cm.—(Go, Diego, go! ; #10)
"Based on the TV series Go, Diego, go! as seen on Nick Jr."—T.p. verso.
ISBN-13: 978-1-4169-6876-4
ISBN-10: 1-4169-6876-8
I. Villalobos, Ligiah. II. Mawhinney, Art, ill. III. Go, Diego, go! (Television program) IV. Title.
PZ7.I355Gid 2009
[E]—dc22
2008006782

Hi! I am  .
DIEGO

Today we need to rescue

some ocean  !
ANIMALS

The 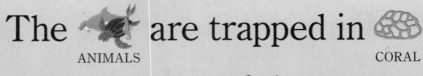 are trapped in 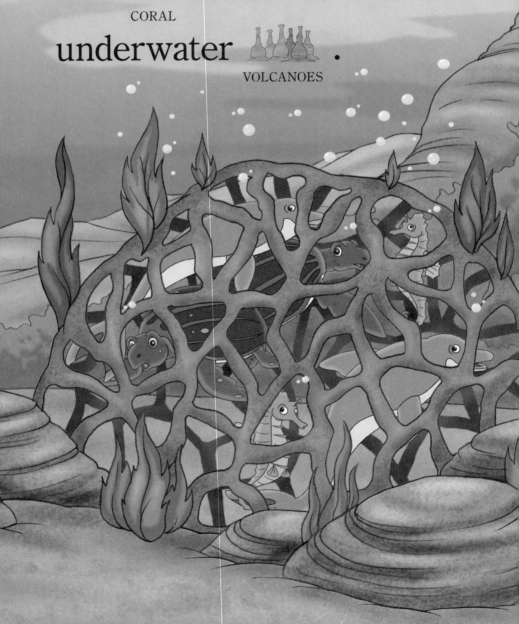 CORAL

ANIMALS

at the bottom of the ocean.

The CORAL is next to some

underwater VOLCANOES .

The  are getting

VOLCANOES

ready to blow!

We need an ocean animal to show us the way to the .

CORAL

 says the animal we need

CLICK

has **8** arms.

EIGHT

Is the animal a , a 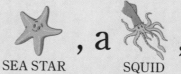,

SEA STAR   SQUID

or a ?

GIANT OCTOPUS

Count the arms to find out.

Which animal has **8** arms?

EIGHT

Right! We need a  !
GIANT OCTOPUS

We have to go under water

to find the  .
GIANT OCTOPUS

We can use my Rescue to find the  .

SUBMARINE

GIANT OCTOPUS

To the rescue!

There is the  .

GIANT OCTOPUS

The  says he will

GIANT OCTOPUS

help us.

Hurry! We have to follow

the  !

GIANT OCTOPUS

Look! The GIANT OCTOPUS can change colors.

He can turn , ,
PURPLE   GREEN

and .
BLUE

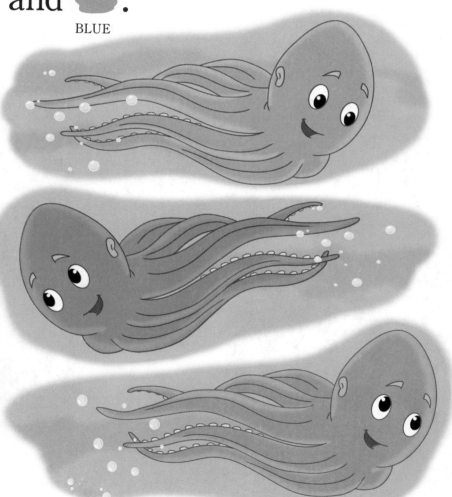

Oh, no! I see some .
WHALES

The  is afraid of !
GIANT OCTOPUS   WHALES

The can squirt
GIANT OCTOPUS   PURPLE

ink to hide from the .
WHALES

The 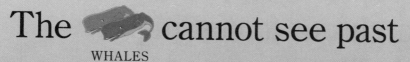 cannot see past

WHALES

the  ink, so the

PURPLE GIANT OCTOPUS

can swim away.

Squirt, , squirt!

GIANT OCTOPUS

Watch out for falling  !
ROCKS

The ocean  will hit
ROCKS

my  .
SUBMARINE

The  can catch
GIANT OCTOPUS

the  .
ROCKS

How many did the

ROCKS

 catch?

GIANT OCTOPUS

Yeah! **8** .

EIGHT   ROCKS

I see the !

VOLCANOES

Do you see the trapped ?

ANIMALS

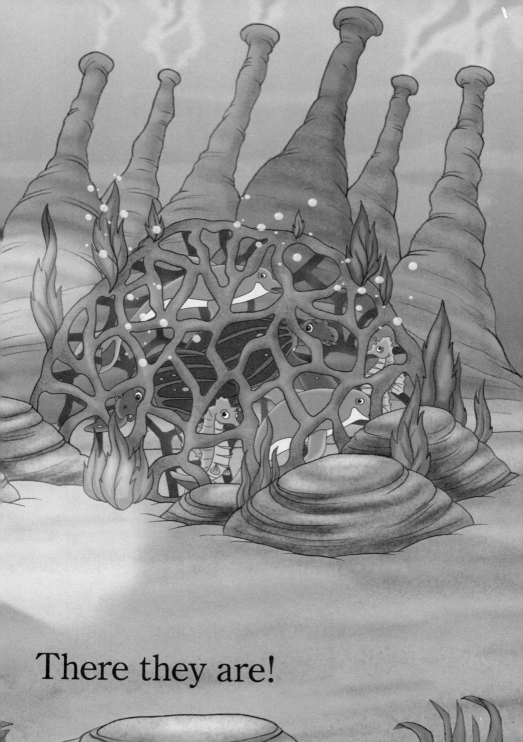

There they are!

The  GIANT OCTOPUS can use his **8** EIGHT arms to dig a hole under the CORAL .

Dig, , dig!
GIANT OCTOPUS

Now the  can swim to safety.

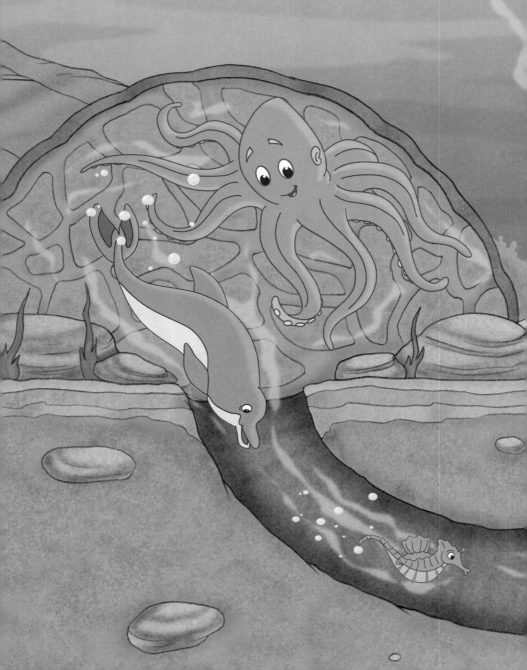

Swim, ! Swim,  !
TURTLES DOLPHINS
Swim, !
SEA HORSES

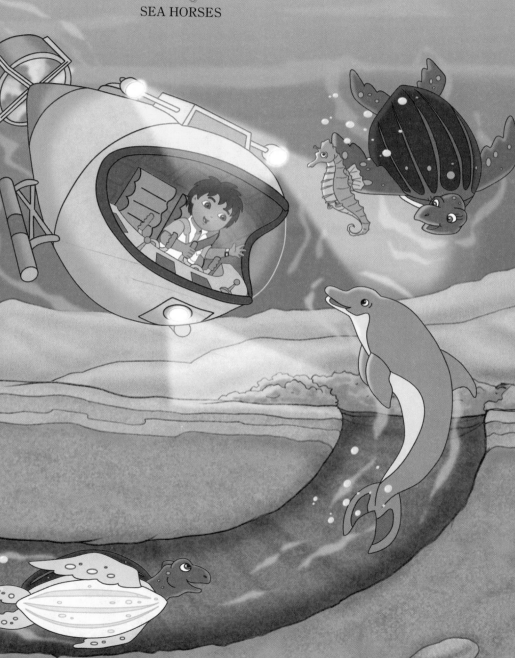

The ocean are safe.
ANIMALS

The  are about to

blow!
VOLCANOES

That was a **blast**!

You were a big help, and so

was the  .

GIANT OCTOPUS

Rescue complete!